For Malcolm, with love

First U.S. edition 2005

Library of Congress Cataloging-in-Publication Data

McMenemy, Sarah.
Jack's new boat / Sarah McMenemy. — 1st U.S. ed.
p. cm.
Summary: When Jack visits his Uncle Jim, a sailor, he finds it difficult to wait out the stormy weather before sailing his new toy boat.
ISBN 0-7636-2477-2
[1. Boats and boating—Fiction. 2. Toys—Fiction.
3. Lost and found possessions—Fiction. 4. Uncles—Fiction.] I. Title.
PZ7.M2272Jac 2004
[E]—dc22   2003066191

2 4 6 8 10 9 7 5 3 1

Printed in Singapore

This book was typeset in Americana.
The illustrations were done in paper collage and gouache.

Candlewick Press
2067 Massachusetts Avenue
Cambridge, Massachusetts 02140

visit us at www.candlewick.com

CANDLEWICK PRESS
CAMBRIDGE, MASSACHUSETTS

Jack's
New Boat

Sarah McMenemy

JACK went to stay with
his uncle Jim for a vacation.
Uncle Jim was a sailor.
He had made Jack a red toy boat.
Jack loved his new boat.
He wanted to sail it right away.

"Can we go sail my boat now?" asked Jack.

"Better wait. It looks as if a storm is coming," said Uncle Jim. "Those waves would sweep your boat out to sea."

Each day
the stormy
weather only
got worse.

Each morning Jack asked,
"Please can I sail my boat today?"

And each time
Uncle Jim answered,
"All the big boats are
still docked, Jack.
Let's wait for a
calmer sea."

All Jack
could think
about was
sailing his
new red boat.

But each day
was windy
and wet . . .

and the sea still crashed against the shore.

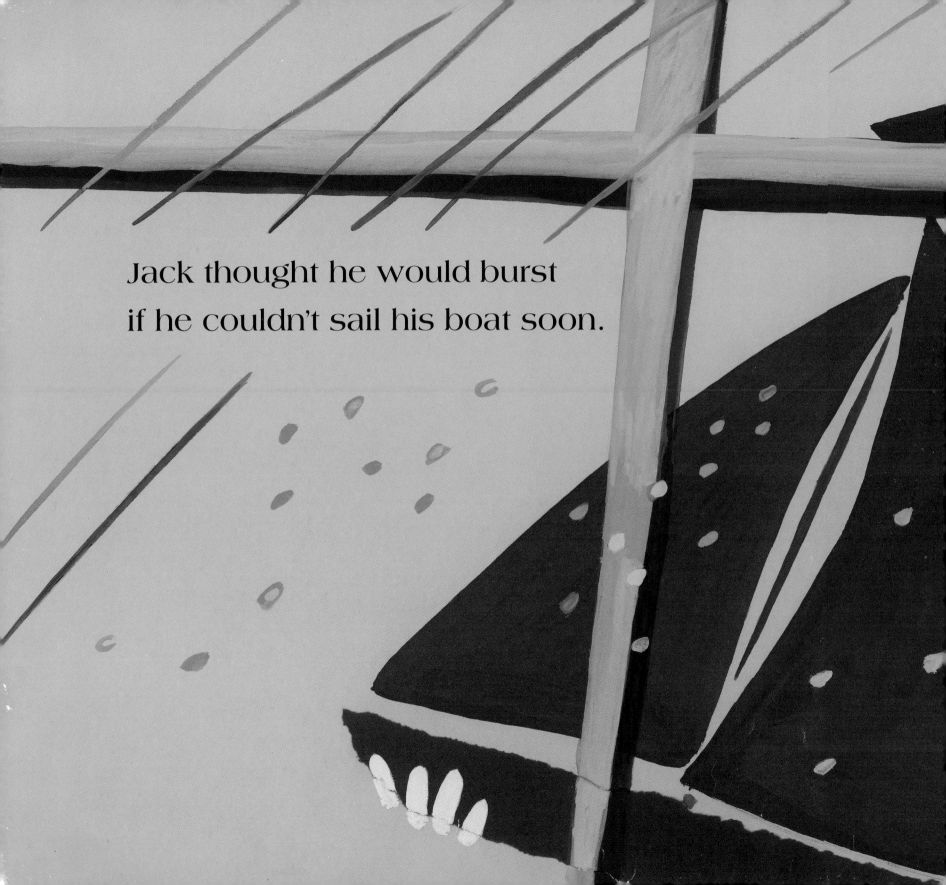

Jack thought he would burst
if he couldn't sail his boat soon.

Still the rain
came down.

Until at last . . .

it stopped!

Jack picked up
his boat, raced out
of the cottage, and
ran down to the beach.

The waves
were still
very big.

I'll just put it in
at the edge of
the water,
thought
Jack.

Then I'll let it go for only a moment.

Jack watched it bob up and down on the waves.

"Not too far," he called as the boat bobbed out of reach.

But the little toy boat drifted
farther and farther out to sea.
"Come back! Don't go!"
cried Jack . . .

as the boat tipped
and disappeared beneath
a giant wave.

"Uncle Jim, Uncle Jim!"
cried Jack. "I've lost my
boat—a big wave took
my boat!"

"Let's go and see if
we can get it back,"
said Uncle Jim.

They walked along the beach for hours,
searching, but couldn't find Jack's new boat.

"Let's go home now," said Uncle Jim. "It's getting dark.
We'll look again in the morning."

but they couldn't find the boat anywhere.

They searched again along the beach . . .

The next morning was bright and sunny. It made Jack feel hopeful.

Then Jack saw something red . . .

but it wasn't his boat.

"I wish I'd waited for the weather to change," Jack said sadly.

"Do you think we'll ever
find my boat?" asked Jack.
"I don't know," said Uncle Jim.
"I hope so.

"Let's do something else
for a little while to cheer us up," he said.
"Let's go and look at the big boats in the harbor."

Sure enough,
Jack cheered
up when he saw all
the colorful boats
lined up along the pier.

He shouted out the colors as he passed.

"Green, white, orange, yellow, green, blue, yellow, red . . . RED!"

Jack ran to look.

"It's my boat!" he shouted.

"I found my new
red boat!"

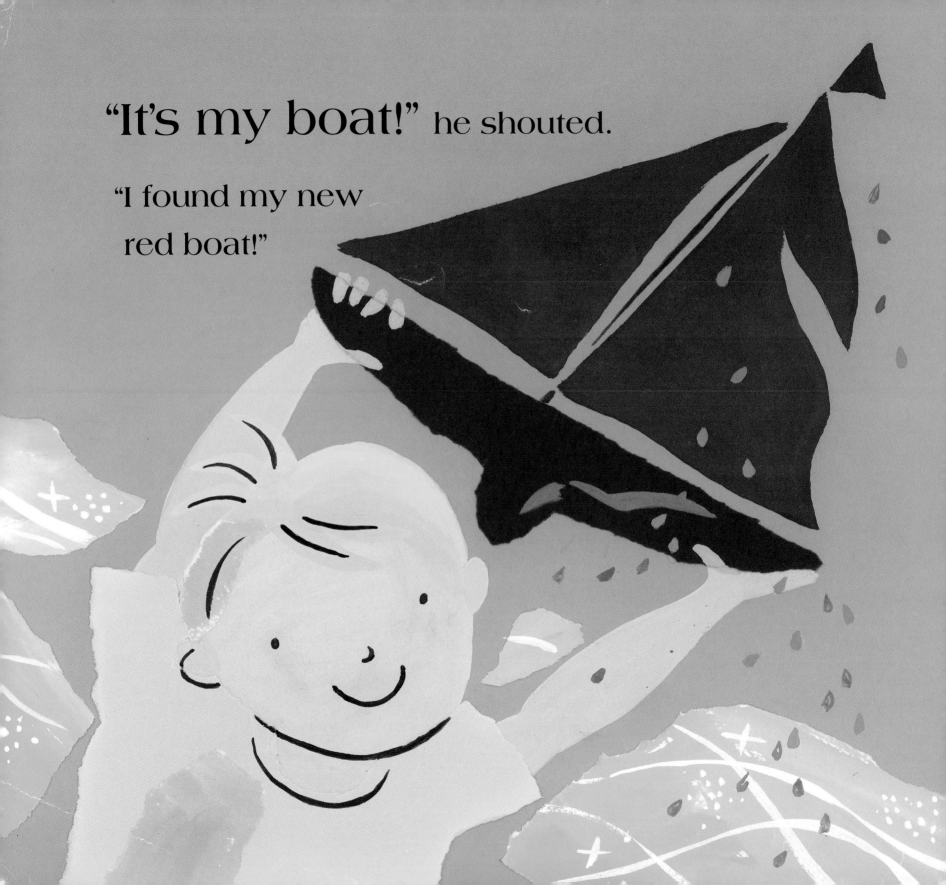

"Can we fix it?"

"Aye-aye!"
said Uncle Jim.
"We'll make her
seaworthy again."

And that's just what they did.